ANOTHER NAME FOR AUTUMN
Corrie Greathouse

Copyright © 2013 by Corrie Greathouse

ISBN-13: 978-0615734767
ISBN-10: 0615734766

Edited by Kimberly Sadler
Artwork by Mark Smith

Printed in the U.S.A.

BLACK HILL PRESS
Contemporary American Novellas
blackhillpress.com

Black Hill Press is a publishing collective founded on collaboration. Our growing family of writers and artists are dedicated to the novella—a distinctive, often overlooked literary form that offers the focus of a short story and the scope of a novel. We believe a great story is never defined by its length.

Annually, our independent press produces four quarterly collections of Contemporary American Novellas. Books are available in both print and digital formats, online and in your local bookstore, library, museum, university gift shop, and selected specialty accounts. Discounts are available for book clubs and teachers.

To my mother, Joan Wellman, and everyone who ever taught me how to love.

The leaves don't change in Los Angeles.

01

The leaves don't change in Los Angeles. At least, the ones outside my window don't. In three years they haven't changed. Not once. The trees bear fruit, most of it falling to the ground—the gardeners have to move it before they can cut the grass. On Wednesdays, I try to wake before they arrive, the gardeners—with their mowers and radio-static mariachi. They laugh loudly. I like that about them. For three years I've lived here and only recently did I notice they always come on Wednesday. I don't know why they were here this afternoon. It isn't Wednesday. There was no music. No mowers. But I saw them from the window while I was looking at the leaves.

Your book of dreams, what sort of paper was it typed on? Did you use the same sort of paper for each dream? Did you type them in the middle of the night, or wait until morning came? Do you still record your dreams? Do you sometimes forget about them until some moment strikes you in the afternoon, some stranger smiles and suddenly you think, *oh yes, last night I dreamt*?

That used to happen to me.

There is something I need to write that contains the words: 'three years is a long time between *I love you*s.' That is all I know about it right now. I haven't been writing much lately. I don't paint anymore either. There is a piece I pull out from time to time. Something I started a long time ago.

One night at the end of autumn, just before winter arrived, I came home—I was living in New England then on an acre of land surrounded by trees, amidst gardens I would plant in spring, and summer black raspberry bramble I would wade into, flinching when the bramble poked through my overalls while I was picking berries for friends. There weren't any berries that night. There weren't any friends. It was cold and I was lost. My spacebar was broken so the first line looked like this:

"when.all.else.fails...run."

I still love that line. That story still begins that way. The beginning of that story is the only thing that hasn't changed over the years. I was younger then. The ending has changed again and again. I'm not sure how it ends anymore.

Something about freedom.

I forget right now. I forget a lot of things. When I saw the gardeners this afternoon, for a moment I thought it was Wednesday. For a moment I was in New England waiting for the leaves to change.

But then I heard the children playing next door and the baby crying downstairs. They aren't my children. I don't even know their names but they all have brown hair. The girl wears hers in braids. From my window I can't see the color of their eyes but I imagine they are blue, like mine. The house is colonial brick and belongs to the grandparents. The grandfather toils slowly, working in the yard on Sundays, tending a mostly dead lawn while the children sing and play some adaptation of London Bridge beneath a half-rusted white wrought-iron lattice that has never moved. Year in, year out the children grow and the lattice sits, an aging bridge of London waiting for a wedding, a holy union that hasn't happened yet.

The mother lives there too. Some mornings, in the moments just before sunrise, when I'm in my kitchen having tea and writing letters, I smell the smoke of her green-box cigarettes drift through my windows. I stand to close them and watch her for a moment before she slides through the door, disappearing inside. I don't smoke anymore. I never see her play with the children.

I don't have any children, but I imagine if I did I would play with them—that we would sing songs, and we would dance and I would tell them about the world. I imagine that I might write them letters and maybe they would call those letters stories. Since I was a girl I've been writing letters in the morning, but I've never written a morning letter to a stranger before. This isn't like other mornings; that must be why this isn't like other letters.

02

The day I left for New England, it hadn't rained in Los Angeles for months. Even the day I buried my mother, the sun shined as though my heart shouldn't be so sad. I turned my head toward it and opened my eyes. They say you're not supposed to stare at the sun but I thought maybe if I looked at it long enough, it might fill the holes in my heart with warmth. Something seems the matter with a funeral on a sunny day. Something seemed the matter with most things that day.

Every day after that was the same. I think that was the day I started to disappear. I didn't cry. Something seems the matter with not crying when the person who loves you most dies. When the person who gave you life and on whom you depended for all of the things that kept you alive, dies, and leaves behind a child, the child dies a little bit too. Even if they aren't a child anymore.

That was a long time ago. I used to think that was why I went to New England, because if I stayed in Los Angeles I was going to dissolve.

When people go away, pieces of your heart fall out and there are holes where that person used to be. No matter how fast you move, those pieces always fall out. All you can do is try to pick them up and gather them into a mosaic—but you can never put them back in. Once pieces of your heart fall out, the shape of you changes and even if you pick them all up you can't put them back.

I didn't know what to do with the broken, mosaic pieces of my heart. I thought I would find the missing parts of myself in the seasons.

I thought if I left Los Angeles, the pieces of my heart would stop falling out and I would be safe, that the winter would keep me from dissolving, spring would warm my heart, and the very best parts of me would come back to life.

It was spring when I left. I found a house in New England. My house was green, paler than the trees and almost hidden. The yard was overgrown with black raspberry bramble and alone against a solemn web of bare tree limbs waiting their turn to come back to life. The paint was peeling on the outside and the driveway wrapped around like a hug from the familiar road. The first time I saw it, the inside was empty save for an easel tucked inside of a closet. I think that's how I knew it was mine. I think the landlord knew it was mine, too. He saw me smile when I looked at the easel and said he didn't remember seeing it before but if I wanted to live in the house, the easel could be mine, too. For seven days, I stayed inside. I watched the blooms, I watched the trees come back to life. I used to say it had something to do with God and creation. The truth is, I don't know why it was seven days. Seven seems to have a lot of meaning to people. I wonder what it means to them and if that's because of God. I want everything to mean something. To me, everything does mean something. I want everyone to be like me.

03

I was sleeping in the middle of the day. I had a dream that the empty room in New England was filled with canvas and I was painting portraits of people I had never met but who all had the same smile I did and everything meant something to them, too.

When I woke I walked into town, watching the flowers along the way. There was a small art supply store and an empty young girl who worked there for her parents. I walked in and I stared at her. I imagined what she looked like when she smiled. I stayed there a long while. I think she thought I would steal from her. I have never stolen anything. I have wanted to, but if you take something that isn't given to you, it isn't really yours anyway. Sometimes you want something and you just don't know how to ask for it.

I bought canvas and paints and brought them home. I set them in my empty studio and poured a glass of wine. I set the canvas on my easel in the corner between the windows and sat on the floor. I stared at it for a long time. I closed my eyes and saw the mosaic pieces of my heart—I almost cried.

When my mother died, I didn't cry. I was afraid and thought I might never stop; that my tears would fill the holes in my heart and I would drown—I was afraid I would die too.

Sometimes, my heart fills with so much *everything* I think it might explode. I put my hand over it to keep all of my feelings on the inside where they are safe. When you let them out, you give them to people and when they leave, they take pieces of you with them. They know your insides and you can't make that go away. It is safer inside, and you can't let *everything* in.

That afternoon, when I closed my eyes and saw the mosaic pieces of my heart, I knew I wouldn't drown. I painted every day. I filled the canvas with my dreams. I filled my pale green house with portraits of people who had smiles like mine. When Finley came, my heart overflowed and filled my house with love.

At the end of spring, I had a dream about music. I had a dream that *everything* made sense. That was when the man from the restaurant gave me the piano. I had a dream that I was sleeping in my too-dark room and woke to a piano song. I didn't have a piano then and had never heard the song before but I knew it was about me because it sounded like my name. In my dream I was wearing the white slip I only paint in, for sleeping.

I walked into the studio and painted the dream where *everything* made sense. I painted the song that sounded like my name. I painted the things that would overflow from my heart if I stopped putting my hand over it. The painting was yellow and it was blue. It was red and it was black. It was sunset and sunrise and everything that happens when your heart overflows.

When I was done, I didn't leave the painting on the easel to dry. I hung it on the wall in the library. Some of the colors dripped onto the floor. I took refuge on the cool floor beside them and I went back to sleep.

When I woke, I walked into town. I sat on a bench in the park and noticed the man from the restaurant in the distance. He was walking along the path circling a small pond with a footbridge. There was a peace about him and so I followed and sat on the footbridge to see my reflection in the water. I heard the swishing of arms against the body of a rough coat as he came around again, and turned my head. I shielded my eyes from the intensity of the sun while he silently eclipsed its focus. I saw the shape of the man but the sun kept his features hidden. He said hello and I smiled. I don't know if he smiled too but he asked if I knew I had colors in my hair and on my arm. Of course, I told him. I had been painting a dream I had about a piano and a song that sounded like my name.

I told him I had painted sunset and sunrise and everything that happens when your heart overflows. He told me he played the piano when he was young; that there was a woman who loved dancing almost as much as she loved him. He told me that he played the piano so she could dance because he couldn't love her back and wanted to give her something. He told me how one day when he was playing the piano for her, she stopped spinning for a moment and he saw her eyes. He stopped playing and told her it was time to go now and she shouldn't come back. He said that was the only loving thing he had ever done.

He told me he still had the piano; it was out of tune and hadn't been loved for a very long time; that the keys sometimes stuck, and that its tone changed with the seasons. He told me that when you neglect something for a very long time it changes.

Did you know that if it is cold, the sound of a piano changes? The sound becomes dampened. The strings are cold and stretched and the soundboard sometimes cracks. When the soundboard cracks, the piano is mostly broken. You can fix it but it is very expensive and there aren't many people who know how; when you don't play a piano for a long time, it falls out of tune. The strings loosen and the intervals between the sounds expand. The space between the beautiful sounds and movement of the keys expands; you have to let the piano settle into its environment before it will be beautiful again.

I asked him if I could have the piano.

He brought it to my house in the back of an old truck, and brought along a man I always saw working in the café in town. The man from the café asked me how long I had been playing the piano. Forever, I told him. I don't know if he knew I was lying but telling him that seemed easier than telling him that somewhere there was someone who wrote music that sounded like my name—*that* someone was my forever and I was his and the piano belonged to him. I was merely attending to it, brushing away neglect, in his absence. He said he had always wished he could play the piano.

When I was a girl, my mother made me take piano lessons. I think because she wanted me to learn to make music; I think because she wanted me to be like her. Until just this moment, I had forgotten my mother loved the piano, that maybe that was why she wanted me to play. She wanted me to love something she loved. I remember her playing in the church when I was very small. Not during a service, just one Sunday morning, off in the corner with the piano, playing and smiling quietly to herself. She had a beautiful smile. I wonder if that memory is real or something that my heart created so that things would make sense. My heart does that.

04

It was the beginning of autumn in New England; the days when the temperature drops slightly and somehow the sky is still kissed by traces of summer. The birds haven't left yet and August sunshine sits around the bend with warm summer thunderstorms behind her. I love the rain in summer. It comes unexpectedly. The best things come unexpectedly.

I was standing on a sanded-concrete gallery floor watching photographs on the wall. The world through the eyes of one called Finley. I always wonder what a photographer thinks in the moment they see an image and want to hold it forever. I wonder what it was about that moment that made them hold on. On the east wall was a colorless, unframed image of a bench. Concrete. Near, but not on, a street corner, next to a mailbox and a parking meter. There was no one in the photograph. No person passing time, waiting for something to happen. No lovers sitting, backs turned to one another—perhaps after a quarrel or just before a kiss. Just a bench. It was not a stop on a bus line. Not sitting outside of a bakery or café. It was just there. Between a parking meter and a mailbox. Not facing the street, but the sidewalk. Serving no discernable purpose but to provide a place for rest. Or daydreaming. I imagined it was a bench for daydreaming. For those moments when the body needs to pause so the mind can dance alone.

It was the only photograph I saw that day. I went outside to smoke, considering the bench and watching passing traffic. The streets were mostly quiet, as though the world knew something I didn't and decided to stay home.

Summer storms rumble before they arrive. Autumn storms have their own sound. They are subtle, coming quietly like the changing of the leaves. Somehow, even before they have fallen, autumn leaves change the sound of the rain.

I was smoking and thinking about the bench in the photograph. Smoking and wondering who might have been sitting on it and what they may have been reading and were they smoking too? Wondering how many passers-by had leapt upon its seat—dancing a step or two before bouncing down and continuing on their way. I wondered what those people had been thinking about. Where they had been going. Who they loved and whether that person loved them back. There are a lot of people who never get loved back. Have you ever been loved back?

You can always feel autumn before you can see it. All of the seasons in New England are like that. Except for spring.

Spring is different than the others; spring arrives one day, showing her colors and singing love songs. The air will still be frozen, there will be snow on the ground, but one day while you walk, you hear your first Fox Sparrow song, your eyes drift skyward and discover Almond Blossom, then every day becomes more beautiful than the last. Finley was like spring—one day, just there.

It took me a moment to notice it had started to rain.

I turned to watch the gallery through the window, letting the rain fall, holding my cigarette to my lips, if only to keep my thoughts from escaping. Through water-beaded bangs, I watched a girl inside smile. She took a boy's hand and turned her eyes to his, looking up at him as though she could send her thoughts to his mind through her eyes, taking his hand to her lips. He touched the tip of her nose with his scarf and she laughed. I couldn't hear her laugh over the sound of the leaves and the rain but it looked like the kind of laugh that said, *I am happy, you are happy. I hope you know that.*

The gallery seemed so much warmer from outside in the rain, watching water-speckled faces crowd near the photograph of my bench. I am not sure when it became mine. Only that somehow, as I crafted stories about it and the lives that it touched, it became a part of me. I understood. I felt understood. Understanding is a precious thing; one that doesn't come often, and never by force.

My reflection rested on the surface of strangers and the stories of their lives while I searched my own. Then my reflection wasn't alone.

Behind me in the glass stood a water-freckled face, black stalactite hair beneath a parka hood that had been raised a few minutes too late. I stood still, watching the reflection and the rain. Thinking that if I moved just a little to the right, the bag on his hip would look like it was on mine. Thinking that if I stepped my feet just a few spaces apart, his chin would sit atop my head and we would make a totem pole.

I pressed my feet a few spaces apart, so I could see our gallery reflection totem.

—Look, I said

—You're getting all wet, he responded.

I told him it was his job, as the top of the totem, to keep me dry and protect me from the rain. His reflection reached to the bag on his hip, pulled out large photograph rectangles and held them over my head. I turned around to see him.

—Finley, he said.

—Finally! I was getting all wet.

He asked if he could walk me home.

05

The window of my bathroom overlooks an alleyway twenty-seven blocks from the Pacific Ocean. There are a father and son who take a walk every morning. For three years I have watched them from my window on the second floor, sometimes while I am brushing my hair or my teeth; sometimes while I watch my reflection in the mirror and wonder where I went.

The child's hair has grown over the years. It is blonde the way mine used to be when I was small, cut in a similar face-framing bowl that he will resent his mother for when he grows older, though she will assure him it was fashionable. I used to wonder where the father and son went on their walks until one morning I went for a walk of my own and saw them at the café. They sat at a center table sharing a blueberry muffin, the boy tore his half into pieces and swung his too-small-to-touch-the-floor legs back and forth; the weight of his sneakers enough to propel them up and down—toes occasionally catching his father's knee. I watched them for a moment, smiled to myself and walked home. Whenever I see them, I pause and think to myself, *All is right in the world.* I don't think I believe that anymore, but seeing them gives me hope that it is partly true.

I wonder if the child will remember how dearly his father loved him when he was small, or the way they walked every morning. I wonder if he will write letters. When I first began watching them, the boy was so small his father would carry him. He walks on his own now, sometimes they hold hands and sometimes the boy runs ahead. I wonder what they talk about.

I want to walk on my own again with someone to carry me when I can walk no longer. I want to hear someone else's voice. I want to share a muffin in a café. I want to remember.

I have tried so hard to forget.

It is easier to forget in Los Angeles. The seasons mostly stay the same, each day only slightly different than the last. Days move together in sunny eternity; sun dresses in December and children dressed in t-shirts riding bicycles outside on Christmas day. Once, it was the only place I knew. I left alone, searching for some part of myself I thought I might find in the seasons. Some part of myself I thought lived inside the visible passage of time.

Seasons imprint memory in the senses deeper than the sunshine. Sunshine leaves its memory on the surface of skin.

Today, it is raining in Los Angeles. On days that it rains it is harder to forget. On days that it rains, the falling sky and sound of the leaves return me to seasons and a time that was *everything*. A time that leaves me wondering how one lives when all wonder exists in the past.

I let Finley walk me home in the rain. He held his photographs over my head and asked me what I loved.

—Painting, I said.

He asked me if there was anything else.

I told him I loved a lot of things. He asked me what sort of things I loved.

—Dandelions…

—Silly girl loves a weed, he laughed.

—They aren't weeds, Totem Captain, they are wishes…You blow them into the wind and they fall somewhere in the distance and come true when you least expect it, in a place you never thought to look.

I changed my step to a skip and jumped just outside the cover he held over my head. I turned around and smiled and he caught up with me again. He asked me if I loved people. I told him I loved stories and we kept walking. The walk from the gallery to my house was long.

I didn't live in town like the boy and the girl on the other side of the gallery glass. I lived alone in a bungalow house built by a man's hands for his family sometime several decades before. The man's son is grown now and has a family and a home of his own. He rented the house for a reasonable sum and in return I made it a home. I painted each room a different color and named them all. I spent nights sewing curtains for the windows and cushions for my window seat. The room with the window seat was my library and faced my garden. My books stood at attention, housed in wooden wine crates arranged along the walls, stacked high in shapes I changed from time to time.

When I arrived in New England, I wanted to have gardens and spaces to wander and watch seasons pass. To feel all of the things I never knew as a girl.

Finley and I walked in silence listening to the sound of the rain on the leaves and the squeak of pine needles on asphalt beneath our feet. At the base of my drive stood a lamppost covered in ivy. The ivy had grown up and around the post, crawling over the top as though it were extending a hand to the birds asking them not to leave when winter came.

Finley tried to swing around the pole but his hands became lost in ivy tangles and he fell to the ground, laughing. The lamp shook with the memory of his weight and I told him it was not the sort of lamppost that liked dancing. He asked me if I liked dancing.

As we walked up the drive to the porch, I told him I did my best dancing when I was alone; I told him that I did my best dancing when I had a paintbrush in my hand and colors on my arms. I told him my best dancing left colorful footprints on the wood floors of my house. My landlord didn't mind the footprints. He said they made the house look loved.

The screen door to my porch was in disrepair and the right corner of the screen hung down, folded over like a dog-eared page. The husband and wife who lived in the house before me had grown old there together. The steps to the porch had long ago been replaced by a ramp for the man's wheelchair when his bones became too tired to walk any longer. The ramp was always slippery in the rain but I couldn't bring myself to put the steps back. The steps were in the garage with stacks of memories and artifacts of the love that lived in the house before I arrived. I would find their memories in corners of the house, in the most unexpected places. Little memories of a love that was old and strong and true. Love notes that spoke of love by virtue of the fact that they were written at all. She had the handwriting of one who had been well trained in school to use good penmanship, the penmanship of one from a time when it reflected character. I think she must have had a job at some point or spent time out of the house. She left him loving notes pinned to the cabinets in the kitchen. My favorite was one marked "Automatic Oven" where she had written step-by-step instructions on how to use it. When you love someone, you make sure they are nourished.

I used to love sitting on my porch in New England. In the corner was a giant wooden spool for resting my feet and an old chair faded on the side facing the sun, worn with cat scratches, and bursting at the arms with stuffing in search of freedom. The space between them was just enough that I could stretch my sketchbook out across my thighs and propping my knees up, become a drawing table. My chair faced the garage and the woods, the invisible neighbor's house and the sky. The floor was strewn with discarded sketches; their pencil marks marred by rain that leaked through the porch roof and snuck in through the screen when gusts of wind came. The charcoal characters were given new lives and shapes by the storm. Sometimes, I would pick them up again after the rain. I liked what Mother Nature had done so I hung them to dry along the mantle above the fireplace. There was a mirror above the mantle and sometimes I would watch my face change in the flames, wondering if I looked more beautiful by firelight. I paused at the door leading inside, watching my home through the window. I always did that.

06

Does your heart ever create things so that *everything* makes sense?

Sometimes, in Los Angeles, when I am up before the sun and the world is silent, I write letters and my heart pretends Finley is sleeping in the bedroom and soon he will wake and ask me who I am writing letters to. In my heart, I laugh and tell him I am writing a letter to my forever and has he seen him? In my heart, he laughs. He kisses me and asks me what this mystery man looks like and says he will not give me up so easily. I tell him my forever is the handsomest man I ever saw and I don't ever, ever want him to.

In my heart, when the world is silent, Finley is still with me.

My mother would have been glad the sun was out when we hid her from it. She always loved the sunshine. I think that is why she always smiled, even when it wasn't sunny. When I was a girl, we would sit outside in the park near our house. I would spin around in circles, staring at the sky, making wishes until my little girl balance could no longer hold me standing. I would fall and we would laugh and I would ask her to tell me a story.

I have always loved stories. I wonder if the boy's father tells him stories. I imagine that he does and that sometimes the boy spins around making wishes until he falls. I imagine when he falls that the ground beneath him is soft and he laughs. When you are grown, you mostly stop spinning and looking at the sky, but you still make wishes and you still fall. When I fell, the ground was not soft beneath me. I was broken and some of the ground was broken too and it became a part of me. It was hard and parts were jagged and some of them went beneath my skin.

When pieces of your heart fall out, they do not leave soft edges—they are jagged and hard and when you let someone in you have to be careful or you will cut them on the edges of holes that someone else left. The day Finley left, the sun was not shining. I was not spinning but I fell through the holes of my own heart.

I don't remember my father. Yet I have painted him and made stories about his life and the sound of his voice. I have written him letters. Some of the stories my mother told me, and others I made up myself when I was small. It's hard to know which are which anymore. That's the thing about memory. That's the thing about stories and daydreams and the places we hide while we wish the world were different. I sometimes forget which of them are real and which are stories I discovered in the night or in a daydream, or saw in a bird as it was flying away from home, or which stories were created by my heart so that things would make sense. Sometimes I forget what is real. Do you ever forget what is real?

Once, I saw three birds on the telephone wire outside. I watched one of them fly away by itself toward the Pacific Ocean. I sat, waiting to see if the bird would come back but before that happened, the other two flew away, the other way, toward the city.

I sat for a long time, staring at the place on the wire where the birds had been, wondering if the ocean bird would come looking for the others or if they would come back and wait for it. I imagined the wire was their home. None of the birds came home but I have committed their wings to memory. I make stories about the ocean bird and the city birds. I imagine they found each other somewhere; that the city birds came back. That maybe they went far away and the ocean bird searched and searched for them, flying from one end of the sky to the other until he found them again. Some days I see a bird flying, recognize its wings and wonder if it is the ocean bird or one of the city birds or if my stories have made them unrecognizable. I will see them everywhere because they became a part of me in the moment before I watched them fly away.

It is twenty-seven blocks from my apartment to the ocean. In three years, I have never seen it.

When I was a girl, my mother told me stories about when she met my father in the clock shop. I would ask her if he was handsome. Yes, she would say. He was the most handsome man she ever saw. I would ask her about the things he made and how he made them. She would tell me he created the most beautiful clocks she had ever seen.

She would tell me he used his dreams to make the clocks; that he put his dreams inside of time. I would ask her where he put his love then. She said he gave that to me. She said he put all of his love in my heart and that is why I sometimes feel like I have too much. She would tell me his heart was big and full of love and that was why my little-girl heart felt too small sometimes. I would smile and ask her if he made gold clocks. Yes, she would say. The most magical gold clocks that ever were magical. I would tell her that is because love is made of magic. I would ask her when my father was coming home.

He isn't coming home, she would say.

Whenever she would say that, she would reach out her hand to touch my heart. Sometimes, when I am out for a walk, I see my mother's hands, then look up and see the face of a stranger.

I think the first wish I ever made was that my father would come home. I still make wishes about people coming home. Some days it feels like no one is coming home ever again. I stare at the doorknob and watch the window. I listen for the sound of footsteps on the stairs. I close my eyes and sometimes I hear Finley say, *magic*.

07

The first time I ever wrote a letter to my father was one year just before Christmas came. I wrote a letter asking him when he was coming home and where he was and if he was making beautiful clocks there too. I asked him if it snowed there. I asked if he missed me. In my little girl dreams, wherever he was, he wanted me to be there too and every day he missed me as much as I missed him. In my little girl dreams, when he saw grown-ups spinning children around in the air, he looked at his empty hands and felt sad.

When I was small, Christmas was the most exciting day of the year. Waking up full of energy and excitement, running downstairs to a giant tree filled with colorful mysteries waiting to be unwrapped. The first Christmas my father was gone we didn't have any money. We didn't ever have much money once he was gone. My mother bought a two-foot-tall plastic tree and we set it on the end table next to the sofa. I didn't know where to mail the letter and so I left it under the Christmas tree and hoped Santa would take it to him. When I woke Christmas day, the letter was gone and there weren't any big, colorful mysteries under the tree; there were two rectangular packages. I didn't even need to open them to know what they were, a coloring book and markers. I spent all day coloring the pages of that book with marker, watching the colors bleed through to the other side, tearing them out and taking them to my mother, announcing "I made you something!" every time. She asked me if maybe I didn't want to save some of the pictures to color another day but I told her I was full of so much love I wanted to give it all to her right away. She laughed and asked what would happen then. I twisted up my face then I smiled and said, "I'll make more."

That was the year I learned about giving. That was the year I learned that things aren't important. That it isn't what you give or how much you have, unless you're talking about love. When you love someone, you do the best you can. You give them everything in the world and you give it from your heart, even if everything in the world doesn't look like much at all. When something comes from your heart, it doesn't have to be wrapped in colorful paper with sparkling bows to be beautiful. When something comes from your heart, people know, and when you give—you never ever run out.
Until just this morning, I think maybe I had forgotten about the last part.

08

I don't watch the inside anymore. I watch the outside now, from my window most days. Most days I am awake before the sun in Los Angeles, watching everything but the shadows remain the same. Today is not like other days. That must be why it is raining.

In New England it rains all of the time no matter what the season, but the autumn rain was always my favorite. I don't know whether I loved it best before Finley came or if that's what happens when your heart falls from the sky. When Finley walked me home and I opened the door to my pale green house, we sloshed inside and autumn rain was my favorite. My clothes were dripping wet, sticking to me, creating odd shapes with my body. Finley took off his parka and hung it on the coat rack in the mudroom. We sat side by side on the bench, making puddles on the wood floor and removing our shoes and socks. I hadn't invited him in. He just came.

I don't invite people into my home in Los Angeles, and nobody comes. The rain has subsided for the moment. There is an umbrella on my porch as though someone just left and will return before the rain is over, or perhaps I will use it to meet them in the park and we will play in the puddles and dance on the bridges. I am not sure where it came from. I haven't been to the park in months. I had a dream the other night that someone was here with me, so close to the ocean. We weren't talking and I couldn't see them but I knew that I was no longer alone.

When I left Finley in the mudroom and went into my bedroom to put on dry clothes, it was like that. I knew I was no longer alone. I left him sitting on the unfinished wood bench with our puddles. I turned up the heat on my way into the kitchen and set the kettle to boil.

My bedroom was dark; all of the time. It was painted a deep violet. The curtains were white and sheer and allowed the light in but the violet walls selfishly drank it each afternoon. Even in the summer. I turned on the light in my closet and pulled out a summer dress. Why shouldn't it be summer inside, after all? I dropped the clothes wet with autumn rain through the trap door to the basement. As I closed the door, I opened my mouth to call to Finley that I would be out quickly but I didn't say a word. Before I could speak, I heard music. I heard a song. It was not a song of siren or of piper. It was language between strangers.

Finley was playing the piano in my library.

When I arrived in New England, I was working at a restaurant and a man would come in every week, sit in the window and have a cup of soup. Every week he would come on Sunday. He was tall and thick and his hair was long and almost curly and mostly unkempt. He always dressed in black and seemed the sort of man who might have been darkly attractive in his youth, but youth had gotten away from him and he was alone now. He had taken advantage of his youth and his looks and hadn't learned how to love. We never spoke. Until the day I asked him about the piano. He hadn't any use for it anymore. I didn't play the piano but someone I loved did and they would fill our home with music. I would listen to them fill our home with music and I would paint.

I wasn't in love with anyone then, but I had this love that was light and spirited and heavy and true and it belonged to someone.

Have you ever seen anyone on the street who was walking alone, yet looked like they were holding someone's hand—their fingers stretched slightly, curled at the tips—the distance between them just enough to fit another hand? I used to hold my hands over the keys of my piano when I would step away from a canvas. I would hold my brush between my fingers and stand behind the bench, stretching my arms out in front of me toward the keys. I would imagine my love fit in the space on the bench between the keys and me. I would hum a song I imagined was mine. I would put the tip of the brush in my mouth and twirl about the room in the white slip I loved for painting. Have you ever seen someone standing on the opposite side of the street and thought: *their hand would fit that space*, then wanted to call to them, *I see the hand that yours is open for*? Have you ever wanted to show them? You can't ever show anyone. If something is yours, you have to be the one who sees it.

When I walked out of my bedroom and saw Finley sitting at the piano, camera still over his shoulder, playing and humming along, I didn't even need to pick up my brush to know that if I tucked it between my fingers and extended my hands over his shoulders toward the keys, that his shoulders would touch the part of my arm above my elbow, that if he turned his head right and tilted it just-so, the tip of his nose would rest in the crick of my elbow and I would feel his eyelashes on my arm.

He didn't look up. I joined him in his hum and walked into the kitchen. I painted the kitchen a steel grey when I moved in. Most of the rooms in that house were dark. I'm still not sure why I did that. I didn't have much color in my life, and only dressed in three. I painted with more but that was because my paintings were where I put all of my hope. Painting was the only time I ever wore white; no one knew I did that. Sometimes when I would paint at night, I would see the light on in my neighbor's kitchen and think they were watching me. I would self-consciously adjust the straps on my painting slip, thinking I didn't want them to see me. I don't think they were looking. But when I saw them through the windows, I couldn't help but look. I couldn't help but wonder if it was warm in their home and what dinner smelled like in their kitchen.

I stood in my kitchen looking at the two mugs on the counter top, counting them over and over: *One, two. One, two.* Moving the tips of my fingers from one handle to the other and over the rims of them both in time with the melody Finley played on my piano. I hadn't even noticed the kettle had begun to whistle. I don't always notice things right away. I was still humming and counting when I noticed the music had stopped. I was still humming and counting when I felt Finley behind me. I heard him laugh and I wondered if I had been counting aloud. He asked me what I was doing and I told him I was making a memory. He said he liked the way I said that and asked me if I did that often. I turned off the kettle and filled the two mugs.

—All of the time, I said.

I handed him mug two and he asked me if that was what painters do, make memories. I asked him if maybe memories weren't the work of photographers and perhaps dreams the things that painters make. He asked me why I was a painter then, if I liked making memories so much. I watched my feet on the floor and told him painting gave me a place to put my dreams.

I smiled.

He took my picture.

He told me he had never seen a smile like that.

Today, I wonder what that smile looked like. What that smile meant. What it said to him and if its voice sounded like mine. Above my stove in Los Angeles, there is a mirror. When I arrived here, I wasn't sure what to put in the empty space that watched me while I cooked so I hung a small white-framed mirror there. When you are alone all of the time, even your reflection feels like company. Sometimes, I look for my smile in that mirror. Sometimes, I tell myself stories or sing love songs. Lately, I just say:

—I want to remember.

This morning I was making tea and listening to the rain. This morning I was standing in my living room, looking at my books and listening when I heard the tea kettle. I went into the kitchen, lifted it from the stove, and caught a moment of my face trapped in the mirror's frame. I remembered

Finley's laugh and I remembered my smile. I remembered that day in the rain.

Have you ever listened to the sound of the rain for a very long time? You can hear it gather. If you are quiet and you listen with your heart you can hear the sounds of the rain change as the cracks in the pavement fill, as the divots in the grass become puddles, and as the flowerbeds turn to mud. You can hear the way the rain changes things. I used to think the rain was sad until one day I listened to the rain for a very long time and I realized it was just like love. Things become full, sounds become deeper, and sometimes, you will hear a bird.

09

When I lived in New England I tried to learn the songs of the birds. The only one I was ever able to recognize was the song of the Mourning Warbler; its song is high and rings vibrato. The Warbler sings then pauses and sings again. When I would hear the Warbler pause I would pretend I could respond to it. I would return its call then pause, waiting for it to sing again. I never thought it sounded like it was mourning at all. Maybe that is why I was able to remember it. Its name was so different from its song.

I asked Finley what song he had been playing on my piano.

—It doesn't have a name, he said.

—Everything has a name, I told him.

— And yours is a song.

He smiled and walked into my library.

When I left Los Angeles, I left most of my things behind. When you are disappearing, your strength disappears too. I didn't have the strength to carry the weight of things, and of my heart. I brought a large, hard-bound copy of *The Velveteen Rabbit* that my mother had given me when I was small. Inside, my name was written in the clumsy, little-girl scrawl of my childhood. If you look closely, you can see the places where I pressed the pen down a little bit harder, trying to craft the shapes that spell my name. That book was the beginning of my love of them. The beginning of a love is always full of magic.

When I arrived in New England, I sometimes went for walks and would see yard sales along the road. I would always stop and look at the things people didn't want anymore or the things someone they love left behind. I would sift through the stacks of books selling for a quarter. Sometimes, I would find pieces of myself, the books I loved and someone else loved too. I would wonder about the things we had in common and the parts of a book that lived inside of them. When you love a story, parts of it live inside of you and can never leave. You get to keep them forever. I wondered if we shared the same parts on the inside. I filled my arms with the things I was and the things I wanted to be one day, and I brought them home. I lined the walls with them and created a library of my heart.

I sat where he had been on the bench in front of my piano and watched him walk about the room, looking at my books and pausing at the window seat. I told him I had sewn the cushions myself. He touched them. He asked me about my books. There were hundreds. Their bindings were colorful, some worn to pale and pastel, some torn and some showing thread, each of them loved. He wanted to know where they came from, and had I read them all?

—Most of them.

—And the others?

—Someday...

He lifted one from the shelf and read the first line.

—"Call me Jonah. My parents did, or nearly did. They called me John."[1]

He read it dramatically as though my worn wooden floors were the stage in a theatre and I was one hundred faces. I laughed and he asked me if this was a "someday" book. I told him it was an any-day book. He said he didn't much like the first line. I told him you don't always like a story from the beginning—that with some stories, you have to be patient. That sometimes, all you know in the beginning is someone's name.

He told me to pick a book.

I stepped to the left of him, covered the binding of the book with the palm of my hand and pulled it from the shelf.

—"Ours is essentially a tragic age, so we refuse to take it tragically."[2]

Finley twisted his face, laughed, and said that was the most boring first line he had ever heard and asked how could anyone read a book like that? He tapped me on the

---

[1] Vonnegut, Kurt. *Cat's Cradle*. New York: Holt, Rinehart and Winston, 1963. Print.

[2] Lawrence, D.H. *Lady Chatterley's Lover*. Florence, Italy: Giuseppe "Pino" Orioli, 1928. Print.

head then reached high and picked another book from the shelf. He opened it and read:

— "We'd seen Milan and Genoa and been in Pisa two days when I decided we'd go on to Florence. Jacqueline made no objection. She never made any objection."[3]

He dropped the book to his waist and looked at me. He looked through me and saw something no one else had ever seen. He spoke to me and said something I had never heard.

— This one sounds like you.

I took the book from his hands, put it back on the shelf and turned to the window. I never told him I almost cried then. I wonder sometimes if I should have. I wanted to tell him *everything*. I've never told anyone everything. I worry sometimes what people will think.

Do you ever worry what people will think? Sometimes, when I go walking in Los Angeles, I see people whose steps seem not even to feel the concrete beneath them, people who smile as though they have always been so beautiful and never known a moment's sadness. I have not always been beautiful. I think some people are born that way and other people become that way over time. When I was a child I was awkward and my spine bent funny. You couldn't see it on the outside; it was only my insides that weren't like everyone else's. The doctors made me a brace to fix my insides and it made my outsides ugly. My brace was a hard shell stretching from my collar to my pelvis. My shell was supposed to straighten my spine; I liked to pretend it protected my heart. When people would say hurtful things I would pretend my shell could protect me. When people would yell, I would

---

[3] Duras, Marguerite. *Le Marin de Gibraltar*. France: Gallimard, 1952 (tr. *The Sailor from Gibraltar*, 1966). Print.

close my eyes and try to make it quiet. Sometimes I wish I had that shell back again.

The book that Finley pulled from the shelf told the story of a woman searching the world on a ship for a man she met once and loved immediately. She was never sure exactly why she loved him, only that it seemed it had always been so. One day he went off and never returned; she began searching for him, port by port around the world and back again. I think these are things people do when they find love. My insides are not like everyone else's.

One thing I have learned is that sometimes people go and you can't bring them back. You have to let them go. You can still love them even though you don't know where they went. Love is like that; it's why people believe in heaven. I didn't used to believe in heaven. I never understood how come only some people could go. I never understood why God only loved some people enough to keep them forever. I believe that when you love someone, you keep them forever. There are all sorts of ways to know that you love someone. I know Finley really loved me because I became beautiful. I believe everyone becomes beautiful when they are loved. I know I really loved him because even when forever came, my heart wanted to keep him.

I walked over to the window seat and ran my hand over its black, velvet-patterned flowers. The flowers were worn from years of standing in this space; I ran my fingers over the worn velvet and watched the seasons change. I didn't say anything until I felt Finley behind me again.

—Yes, that one is like me. No one ever noticed that before.

I watched Finley walk toward the windows in the front of the house. The windows stretched across two walls, four panes high, six across and met at the corner. My easel stood at attention between the sets of panes, waiting for me to dream. I would stand in the window facing my easel, touching the canvas and looking outside at the lamppost. The lamp never worked. Sometimes, on winter nights, I would try to turn the lamp on, pretending I was waiting for someone to come home. I would watch the snow on the steps leading to the front of the house and picture footprints leading to the front door. I always entered through the screen porch in the back. Each year the snow on the front steps would melt, never knowing a footprint, never feeling the weight of someone coming home.

10

In Los Angeles, there is a light on my porch. It works and there is a bulb in it; I never turn it on. It doesn't snow. No one is coming home.

The canvas on my easel was filled with circles atop lines, lines sometimes bent to angles. Finley asked me what they were. Asked me if they were microphones.

—No, I said.

—What are they, then? Are they lollipops? Lollipop dreamer?

—No, they are people.

—Stick people? Like children draw?

—Or people who want to believe we are all the same somehow. I want to believe we are all the same, somehow.

—You are a funny girl.

I didn't know what to say then, so I walked away slowly and began to hum the song he had been playing on the piano. I picked up his tea and carried it to him as he watched the rain from the window. The floors in my house were old and creaked in certain places when you walked. Once upon a time, there had been music in the house and it was recorded. Electrical tape x's were placed in spots where the floors creaked so we would know where we shouldn't step. I had never taken the time to remove them. They had become like scars on the unfinished wood floors. They were there as reminders.

When I came back to Los Angeles, I didn't want any reminders. I put everything in a single box. *Everything* was the sheets of music that Finley made sitting at my piano, rolls of unprocessed film containing moments I wanted to forget, Finley's camera, and your book. Only I didn't know your book was in there. I only learned that this morning when I took the box down from the dark closet it has been sitting in for three years. Three years ago I placed the box on the top shelf, shoved all the way to the corner on the left side so I could forget everything it held. This morning I woke before the sun. I was sleepy and walked into the bathroom to look at myself. I said I wanted to remember, asked myself why I had wanted to forget, then realized I didn't know anymore—that I had forgotten.

I watched the world out of the bathroom window but it was too early for the father and his son to come walking. There was nothing to remind me that all was right in the world. I walked back into my bedroom and the wood floor in the hallway creaked. I don't know if it had always creaked but I know that this morning was the first time I noticed. I opened my closet to find my favorite sweater. I wear it on days my skin feels too thin. It is my grown up shell and it is black.

In the closet in my bedroom there is a window. I don't understand why. It is not a closet large enough to have once been a room. It has never been anything but a closet. I asked the woman whose father built this place with his hands. She doesn't know either. He didn't put a light in the closet, so I think maybe he put the window there instead. The window doesn't provide light anymore. It may have at one point but now the neighbor's tree has grown so large it covers the sun. This morning I pulled my sweater from the closet and put it on over my bones. I looked up and to the left and saw the box full of everything I wanted to forget when I arrived in Los Angeles. This morning I was sleepy and tired of forgetting.

I remembered when I brought Finley his tea he smiled and asked me if I wanted to watch the rain with him. I asked him if we could pretend it was spring. He told me we could pretend anything we wanted. He asked me what I wanted. I told him I wanted *everything*, of course.

—*Everything* only comes one thing at a time, he said.

Then he kissed me.

His lips were soft like the things I couldn't say. I looked to the floor and wiggled my toes. I looked up and asked him if he would please kiss me again. He laughed, took my picture and told me he would kiss me every day until forever.

I told him if today was spring then we should have a picnic, indoors, of course, on account of the rain.

I went into my bedroom and pulled the giant blanket from the bed, my thin arms becoming tangled in its mass and my legs tripping over it as I returned to the library. I dropped the blanket in the middle of the room where Finley spread himself atop the rumpled mess before I could spread it out on the floor. The blanket was violet and nearly matched the walls of my bedroom. I walked around and around, pulling corners out and he pulled them back, both of us laughing.

—You're funny, I said.

—Only to funny girls like you.

—Funny girls like me?

—Yes.

—How will we have a picnic if you won't stop it with the blanket?

—I'll only stop if you promise to let me kiss you again.

—Every day until forever, I said.

And he kissed me again.

I went into the kitchen to make sandwiches, quietly singing a song I used to sing at the park when I was a girl. I only remembered some of the words but singing the ones I remembered made my heart feel light. Sometimes all it takes is a song, a smile, and a place to put your hope.

—What? Finley called, thinking I had said something.

—Nothing, I said and sang a little louder.

On summer days in Los Angeles I hear the brown-haired children next-door singing though I never hear them sing the songs children sang when I was a girl. I wonder if they have ever heard the songs we sang. I wish I could ask them about that, about what children are like now, about why they sing the songs they do and where they learned them. I like to think that songs are like stories passed down and along over years but I never hear the songs I know. I wish I could talk to them about the things children do, what games they play. When I was a child I didn't much like playing outside games. I preferred books. I loved stories and daydreams. I liked to lock myself away inside and experience someone else's world through words. Sometimes the outside world is frightening. Inside, things are nice and quiet. And when you're a child, books almost always have endings where everyone smiles and is happy. Real life isn't like that. I wonder if the brown-haired children know that yet. If I ever get to talk to them, I won't tell them that, about real life and what it's like. I will let them keep their magic for as long as they can.

Do you think anyone ever gets to keep their magic until they are grown? Or when we grow up is there magic only in our dreams? Maybe that is why I spent so many of my days painting. I needed to keep dreaming. I still believed in magic.

After our indoor imaginary springtime picnic, Finley and I fell asleep, full and surrounded by plates. It was not yet evening but the sky was dark from the rain. The violet blanket was bunched from the corners making pillows for our heads on the wood floor. I don't know how long we slept but I know that Finley must have woken first because when I woke, his fingers were touching my hair and he was humming my picnic song even though he didn't know the words. I pretended I was still sleeping, afraid that if I woke, the humming would stop. When I couldn't pretend any longer, I turned my head to Finley, opened my eyes and whispered:

—Magic.

—Magic, he repeated.

And he kissed me.

There are moments in life when suddenly everything makes sense.

I stood up, slipping on the blanket, and walked into the room to watch my canvas and the fireplace. Finley followed me and asked why I had been standing outside in the rain, looking at the photos through the glass. I told him I wasn't looking at the photos. I was watching the stories of the people. I was watching the way they laughed, and their eyes, and I searched their hands for history. I liked that I could see them but I couldn't hear a thing. I told him I had only seen the photograph of the bench. I told him about all of the things I wondered about the bench and the people who knew it. He told me I wondered about people a lot. His eyes moved to the window and I could see them watching the frame, taking in the outside. I wondered if that was how he looked through the lens of his camera. He asked me if I wanted to see his other photographs. I told him I wanted to see the things he remembers.

In his green canvas shoulder bag was a black book, a portfolio holding photographs protected from the rain. The book was large and looked heavy. I sat on the sofa cushion that was on the floor—there was no sofa or frame—only cushions on the ground, always placed where a sofa would be if I were the sort of girl that had a sofa. Finley placed the book in my lap. Its texture was rough, like cracks in a leather sidewalk, or broken, parched ground in a desert. Cracks where something might sprout—if only something could grow there.

I asked him why there were no people in his photographs.

He took my picture.

11

Every day with Finley felt like magic. Sometimes, I watch the days over and over in my mind, searching his eyes again and again. I look at my hands and see his holding them. I look in the mirror and try to see what he saw. Sometimes I smile. Sometimes I cry. Sometimes, I am back in my house in New England, with paint spread on my arms and a brush in my hand while he is playing the piano that was his before he arrived. I look over my shoulder and see his eyes are closed, I watch him make music and say to myself: *that must be because he is dreaming.*

He would play the piano and I would paint my dreams and the things I couldn't say. He always seemed to play exactly what I was feeling. I would ask him how he did that.

—Because I see you, he said.

—I don't understand what that means, I replied.

—You don't always have to understand everything.

I always want to understand everything. I think that is why I imagine things. When I imagine things I can always understand them. When I don't understand things, my heart imagines ways for them to make sense. My heart can never make sense of people disappearing. This morning, when I was walking to the ocean after the bird, I realized that I still believed in magic.

When I left my apartment, the rain had stopped; it was hazy and I was cold. The streets were empty of cars and most of the world had already gone to work. The only people on the street were out for a run or walking their dog. In Los Angeles, people never walk to get anywhere. They walk for health, for entertainment, even for charity, but never to get somewhere. I saw a house with a *for-sale* sign and a little girl's bike in the front yard. I wondered when they were moving and if they knew where they were going. If their new house would be bigger or smaller and if they would all live there together. I don't know if the mother and the father are both there in real life but in my imagination, they are. In my imagination, they are all together and they laugh and play games and go places and the little girl spins in circles and falls down and the ground beneath her is soft. In the yard, the little girl's bike was tipped over as though she had dropped it quickly and gone running in to dinner last night. Her mother will pick it up later. Maybe she lives alone in that house with her mother. Maybe she is like I was. Maybe her mother tells her stories and she wonders where her father went and draws pictures of him in school. Maybe someday she will paint. I hope that she believes in magic.

On my way to the ocean, I walked alongside the fence of a school where the students were out playing. Whenever I see children I search their faces for my own. I think we all do that. Have you ever watched children play? There is always one who stands just a little bit farther away, sometimes looking at the clouds and sometimes looking at the concrete. Sometimes, they look at the other children. Maybe they are daydreaming or maybe they aren't sure they belong there or what they should do and maybe they are afraid. Their voices are soft when they ask questions but when they laugh, it sounds like music. The moments they laugh are the ones when they are not afraid. I love the way it sounds when children laugh. I wish that they would never be afraid.

I have always been afraid.

When I was a child and I walked home from school, I would think of questions to ask my mother. Things I wanted to know about my father and about magic, but it was always dark when she came home and she was always tired so sometimes I asked my questions out loud and sometimes I only asked them in my heart. Sometimes, I would make up stories. They would be my answers and I would imagine they were stories my mother told me.

She would tell me stories about my father and the clock shop. She told me he was an artist, good with his hands; that his clocks were the most precise and their hand-painted faces were the most beautiful she had ever seen. She told me that when I was a baby, she would take me to his shop downtown and he would hold me on his lap while he worked; he would touch the tip of his brush to my nose and I would laugh. She told me he loved me very much. Most of all.

I am still trying to understand the last part.

I don't understand how you can leave if you love someone. My mother told me that sometimes grownups do things they aren't proud of. I always thought that maybe he wasn't proud of me and that was why he wasn't coming home. She said he was very proud of me but that he had the sort of soul that had to wander. I asked her why he made clocks then. She said she didn't know. That he loved to make beautiful things; that he said I was the most beautiful thing he ever made. She said he used to call me his masterpiece.

In New England you can tell time by the sky and the seasons. You can tell time by the color and the sound of the leaves. The leaves don't change in Los Angeles. There are no clocks in my apartment. I don't know what time it was when I closed the door to my car the day I left Los Angeles for New England, but the world was still waiting for the sun and the air was filled with fog and I was disappearing inside of it. When I left for New England, I wasn't sure what I would find there but I thought that maybe my heart lived in the seasons. My heart had fallen out and I wasn't sure where to find it but I thought that maybe it was somewhere hidden in the pageant of time.

When I walked home with Finley in the rain, my heart fell from the sky and came back to me. When I told him about the dandelions, it overflowed and he knew my secrets. He knew I was a dreamer. He knew that I loved to smile and to laugh, and he knew that I had been waiting for my heart. When he followed me inside, he knew he belonged and when he struck the first key on the piano, he knew it was his.

When he was gone, it was summer. It was storming and I was sitting on our porch with the dog-eared screen watching the rain, listening to its sounds and wondering what it was trying to tell me. I stepped outside to feel it and the whole of my heart fell out and drowned in the rain. I went back inside. Has your whole heart ever fallen out? I wonder if Finley's heart fell out, too. I wonder if he knew when he woke that forever had come. I wonder if he knew I would disappear again and that made him leave his camera, if he knew someday I would wonder what my smile looked like and he left his camera to show me, or if he wanted me to remember the moments trapped inside—to keep forever.

There are twenty-four exposures on the film he used. Twenty-four forevers. When I put Finley's camera into the box the day I left New England, I thought it was full. When I opened the box this morning and took his camera out, I held it for a very long time. I didn't take the lens cap off but I ran my fingers over the strap, wrapping it around my wrist and holding the camera to my chest, hoping somehow I could put my heart back in. When I pulled the camera away, my heart was still missing. I looked down and saw that there were three exposures left. That was when I knew my forever wasn't over even though he was gone.

A photograph captures a moment using light, freezing everything forever exactly as it was for a split second of time.

12

A photograph captures a moment using light, freezing everything forever exactly as it was for a split second of time. The way things were for that moment, they can be that way forever. Like magic. When you're a child magic is real. When you're grown you know that nothing stays the same forever. Even photographs. Corners peel and fade, someone sets a cup of coffee over a sunset and a ring sets wet over the artifact of time. The stories you don't see are what I have always loved about photographs. I like to imagine my own stories. I don't have anyone to tell them to anymore, perhaps that is why I write letters. So I feel like I have someone to say things to.

In front of the café near my apartment in Los Angeles, "Michelle + Ryan = Love Forever" is carved into the sidewalk. Written when the cement was wet and now petrified by the sun and time. Every day hundreds of people pass by and I wonder if they think about Michelle and Ryan and how long forever was for them. Every time I walk by I think about them. Sometimes, I walk by the café only to look at their names and hope that they are still in love somewhere. Sometimes, I wish I could travel the world following sidewalk cement love stories and finding the people who made them and asking them how they knew it was forever.

I think some people just know when it's forever. I don't know if it's that way for everyone and I know sometimes people are mistaken. It is easy to become lost that way. It is easy to be wrong about forever when you carry in your heart a photograph of that moment when everything made sense. Has your heart ever become confused by something making sense? Have you ever been wrong about forever? I think sometimes forever makes us wrong by coming too soon.

This morning after I put on my sweater, I returned to the window in the bathroom. The window faces a parking lot across the alley and in the morning I sometimes stand in the window, having tea and wondering things about the people passing by in their suits. The parking lot belongs to a bank. I watch the people get out of their cars and wonder what they think about when they drive to work in the morning, about who they go home to at night and I wonder whether that person, waiting, is happy to see them. I wonder if their heart smiles as they place their key in the door or if they wish there was another place they called home, if maybe they feel the call of another heart that is somewhere far away saying "forever is over here."

Some days I go into the bank when I don't need to so I can see someone smile up close, so I can ask how they are doing and listen to their response. I think it's funny how often people ask how you are doing and don't wait for a response; they don't really want to know. It doesn't matter. Until this morning, I didn't think that anything mattered anymore but I had begun to remember a time when it did. And then I pulled down the box of things I wanted to forget and I found your book. When I found your book of dreams, I remembered that I used to have them, dreams, and I wondered what happened. The only thing that came to mind was that I wasn't sure anymore and I sat down on the floor in the living room near my rug. My apartment is small and in my living room there is a sofa now but no coffee table. I've never had any use for one. In the three years I have lived here, I have never had a single guest. Besides, I need the space to walk and to think, to spread out pages on the floor and write letters. I don't ever send the letters. It's just that there are some things I would like to say, if ever I had the chance.

I used to paint, but I have forgotten how to dream. Maybe it is something about the sunshine here, the way the seasons stay the same and it only rains sometimes. Maybe the rain today is what reminded me of that time I used to dream.

Once, in the afternoon before spring, Finley asked me to tell him about my dreams. I told him I didn't have words to describe them so I painted them instead. I told him to walk around our home, to look at the walls, to flip through the canvases stacked against them and tell me what I dream. He told me that would take forever. I told him at least until spring. He kissed me, then reached for my hand. He asked about my hands that held brushes so loosely one might think they would fall from my grasp. When you hold a dream too tightly you render it quiet; it can no longer speak and be-comes a slave to your hand. Dreams cannot be slaves. The hand is slave to the dream.

    —It is the dream that is alive, I said.

    It is the dream that is alive. Until just now, I had forgotten that I said that. Had forgotten it was true.

13

When my mother was gone, there was a goodbye and there was a funeral. You don't always get to say goodbye. In the morning, when Finley left before it started to rain, I was in my studio and heard his steps toward the door. I jumped up and ran bare footed toward him in my white slip until my heart collided with his chest. He looked down at me, smiling, and put his arm around my waist. I laughed and told him I just needed to know one thing before he left.

—Oh? And what's that, funny girl?

—Do you love me?

—Every day until forever, he said.

—That's an awful long time, I replied.

He asked me if I loved him back. I told him I would write him a love letter while he was gone and that it would be the best love letter that ever was because I loved him more than anyone ever loved anybody else.

He kissed me on the forehead and walked outside.

I worked on my painting for a while longer, then lay on the hardwood floor and wrote him a love letter on parchment. I still remember every word.

"Totem Captain,

Since the beginning of time people have been loving each other. I'd like to say I don't have the words to tell you how much I love you but I do and I say them to you every day. They sound like this: "Good morning."

Every time I say good morning to you, my heart fills with so much love that the only thing I can do is spend the rest of the day giving it to you. I spend the rest of the day filling the corners of our home with my love for you. When I make our tea, it is what fills our mugs and it is your love for me that keeps us warm. I listen to your songs and my heart fills still more and when I sing my made up words, they all mean I love you. When I paint, every color tells the story of our forever. The yellow is when I fall in love with your smile, red, when seasons change and my love takes root deeper than Eucalyptus in the ground, blue is the color of the sky the day we walked in the rain and my heart fell from the clouds and came back to me. I will save other colors for another letter or a song I will sing to you in the morning, but because I know you will wonder, my love, black is when I tell you I love you with my eyes closed. "

I dipped my fingers in paint, yellow and red and blue and black, and one by one I made fingerprint hearts on the page along the bottom where you're supposed to sign your name. I would have signed my name but the day my heart came back to me, Finley told me my name is a song and I don't know how to write music.

When I finished my letter, I folded it in half and set it on the piano's music desk where it would wait until Finley came home, and I went back to painting. Until the day I left New England, the letter sat on the piano. Some days I thought about reading it, but I didn't need to because every word lived inside of me. Some days the rain would fill the ground outside of our home and I would hear it ask: *Do you love me back*? I would look at the sky and whisper:

—Every day until forever, Totem Captain.

I stopped going outside unless it was raining. When it rains, no one can see that your eyes are filled with tears and that your heart is full of holes. When it rained I would some-times sit outside, hoping my heart would fall silently from the sky again and come back to me. Sometimes the rain would sound like footsteps and my full-of-holes heart would flutter. It would feel like Finley was coming home.

The rain takes shape around your body, making you sticky wet. The rain helps you pretend you aren't disappear-ing. I wondered if that was how Finley saw me that day in the rain. I wonder if he knew before we spoke that my heart was full of holes and it would fall from the sky that day and come back to me—that I was his forever and he was mine.

Something happens when someone is gone. It doesn't matter whether there was a goodbye or there was only a funeral. It doesn't matter if the funeral was filled with friends and family or if you were the only person there. When someone who lives in your heart disappears, they take you with them. You go because—more than anything—you don't want them to be gone. You go because you don't want to be alone. When you disappear with them, you get to keep them just a little while longer. The world becomes quiet and their voice is what wakes you instead of the sun. For a long time after Finley was gone, I would wake on New England mornings and reach across the empty space where his body would be too hot when the sun rose and mine would be too cold. I would say "Good morning." I never got to tell him that good morning means I love you. I don't reach across the bed anymore, but when I wake, I still say good morning even though I am alone.

14

This morning I found myself awake before the sun, listening to the songs of the birds. I was thinking something was different about their songs today. I listen to the birds, but I seldom look at them. The birds outside of my window are colorless, with the exception of the occasional shining black crow. This morning, I was standing at the window in the bathroom, with my elbows resting on the window sill, having tea and watching the people, when I noticed a bird on the top of a tree just outside. Its belly was yellow and its wings were black. It was beautiful and it wasn't singing. Why do only the colorless birds sing? This morning when I saw the yellow bird, it was as though I had never seen color before. My heart leapt. The yellow was sunshine bright and captured my eyes. I couldn't move; I stood still in the window, not drinking my tea, afraid that if I moved, the silent yellow bird would be gone and the colorless ones would continue their songs of *something is amiss*. This morning, when I opened the box and found your book of dreams on the bottom, I began to remember.

When I reached my hand into the box, I touched the corners of his sheets of music. I remembered watching Finley take my hand in his and say to me "look at how they fit." I looked down at our hands and told him "not like gloves. That would be too easy to say." I think there are some things that cannot be described. Maybe that is why we have clichés. They help people describe things they can't otherwise understand. I have a lot of questions. There are a lot of things I don't understand. The way our hands fit was not one of them.

When he would play the piano, I would marvel at his hands. I would watch my hands holding brushes and spreading color. I would listen to him make music. The music he made never sounded like songs I had ever heard before. The music he made with his hands was a soundtrack to my dreams on canvas. I remember each song. When he was gone, I would spend hours looking at my paintings, humming the songs he played while I made them. It had become spring. Each canvas had its own song. I couldn't hear the birds.

I don't know how to read music. It is something I have always wanted to do. When I was a girl, my mother wanted me to make music. She told me that I must learn to play the piano and then gave me a choice: I could play the violin or the harp. I was 9. I told her I wanted to play the harp. Because that is what angels do. I told her I wanted to be an angel because angels teach people about love. My mother taught me about love. When I went to my music classes, I didn't understand. My heart could hear the music, my hands would move and want to make it but I couldn't understand the pages in front of me. The symbols confused me. I didn't want to make sense of it that way. I only wanted to move my hands and play what was in my heart. My teacher told me I couldn't do it that way; that I had to learn to understand the symbols. I couldn't understand. I stopped trying to play what was in my heart. Maybe that was why I liked Finley's songs so much. They sounded familiar, like the songs I used to hear in my heart when I was a girl.

This morning, I pulled the sheets from the box and ran my fingers over their lines like Braille, thinking that somehow touching them would tell me which song each page contained. I fanned the pages and they smelled like memories. Have you ever noticed that? How sometimes a scent becomes another time? Are there scents that remind you of your dreams?

I rolled up the rug in my living room and spread Finley's music out on the floor, covering the dark wood and making a carpet from his songs. I thought I had forgotten them. I stepped across each sheet on my tip-toes pretending I was a ballerina. I am not a ballerina.

I stand on my tip-toes when my heart flutters and I am afraid it will fly away, like I have to elevate myself a little bit to catch it; to make sure it stays inside and does not fly out, never to return. I used to stand on my toes when Finley would kiss me. When he kissed me goodbye, my heart flew out. Finley's songs were moving under my feet, around the room while I danced, humming the songs and remembering what it was like to dream. I grew tired. I sat down. There was a fluttering.

I gathered his songs in my hands and put them in a stack again. I set the stack by the window where I watch the children play and I heard the sound of wind chimes. Downstairs, just in front of my balcony, there is a tree that grows peaches and wind chimes. The baby who lives downstairs likes their songs. Some days I cannot tell whether the sound I hear is the wind or the baby playing the chimes. Then I hear him laugh. He plays the chimes better than the wind does. His songs come with magic. When I heard his laughter this morning, it reminded me that I am still alive. When I heard his laughter this morning, I realized I still believe in magic.

I walked back into my living room and pulled the curtains to the side so I could see the baby. His tiny hands were reaching for the chimes. His mother was moving him closer to them then further away, up to reach the tall chimes and down to the low hanging ones. I wonder what will happen when the tree grows fruit and it falls to the ground. I wonder if she will still stand under the tree and hold him so he can make music. I watched her touch her hand to his head and face and I knew that she loved his tiny songs too. I wonder what his songs remind her of. It is the baby's second year here. His mother has lived here always. She is alone, like me. I wonder if she believes in magic.

I decided I would leave the curtains to the side so I could see. I looked at the box in the corner under my easel. I don't paint anymore but my easel stands in the corner, waiting for me. I do not keep canvas on it. There are marks across the frame, lines of color and paint that are left where canvas used to be; a board is there now. Pinned to the board is the first page of the story I began that night in New England.

"when.all.else.fails…run"

That was a long time ago. Three years is a long time between *I love you*s.

I sat down on the floor and put my hands back in the box of things I had forgotten. Among the forgotten things was an unmarked black book. It was not a book printed on a large press. It was the sort of book one makes themselves. The sort of book that one puts together slowly as time passes and they have things they want to say. It was bound by hand and the pages were typed. I had never seen the book before. I don't remember putting it in the box.

When I packed the box of things, I intended never to unpack it.

15

When I moved from New England, I first packed the box and then took my paintings into town. I walked up and down the street through the center of town, looking for people who needed love and giving them what I had left. Some of them smiled, some of them thanked me and some told me to leave them alone. I understood how they felt. Not everyone always wants love. There was a man who asked me what I was doing and why. I told him that in my paintings was everything I had learned and all of the dreams I had left. I told him that I didn't need them anymore.

I went back to my house with the dog-eared screen door.

The great room with the windows was empty. The library had no books left in it. I had set them all out in the rain and emptied our home of everything but the piano. Some things are just too hard to do alone. I sat on the bench and opened the cover. I ran my fingers over the keys. It wasn't my piano anymore. I don't think it ever was. Some things are only yours so that they can be given to someone else. They belong to someone else and it is your job to love them until the one they belong to arrives. Once they belong to someone else, they can never be yours again.

I pressed the "middle c" key on the piano. It was the only one I remembered from when I was a girl. I listened to its song for a moment. I hummed along. I closed the cover and walked toward the lightless, silent lamppost. Sometimes I wonder if the piano is still in the library with no books. I wonder who lives there now and if they have fixed the screen and if they sometimes look at the lamppost when they are waiting for someone to come home. I hope that whoever lives there now knows that someone is coming home.

This morning, when I pulled your hand-bound book from the box, I set it in my lap and looked at it. For a long while I sat wondering what was inside, watching it and waiting for it to tell me a story or a secret, afraid that if I opened it I wouldn't find any answers; afraid that if I opened it, all of the answers would be there. I was afraid, but I opened the cover anyway.

Sometimes, there aren't any answers.

"29 to 31: A Book of Dreams."
I began to read.
I began to think about dreams.
I fell asleep on the floor.

There are sections of your book where for months at a time you do not dream about love and then, three nights in a row, love will find you sleeping. Why do you think that happens? Do you think of love often when you are awake? Do you dream about love when you are in love or only when you want to remember what it was like?

Do you ever try not to dream?

There is a dream in your book where you are talking to a woman you love, whose heart was once yours; where you tell her in front of her family and her new love all that is true, all that she deserves and you say:

"..."I still believe in you'. I close the door. I wonder what they are talking about as I walk across the street. I hope she'll come running out that door and chase after me."

When I read that dream I understood. That dream could have been mine but no one has ever come running, come chasing after me. Once, I thought I heard footsteps in the rain but I was wrong. I still don't know what the sound was; I just know it wasn't that. There has only been one time I said 'I still believe in you.'

There has only been one time that it was true, that is probably why.

16

It was on one of my walks in the rain that I knew it was time to go back to Los Angeles. When I walked into town after Finley was gone, my heart would always take me to the gallery door where I saw his Totem Captain reflection for the first time. The day I knew it was time to go back, I walked to the gallery and when I turned to the door, my reflection wasn't there. That's how I knew it was time. I bought a Los Angeles paper from the newsstand and walked home, using it to shield my head from the rain.

When I got home I spread the sticky wet pages on the floor and began to look. The ink on a newspaper doesn't run when it gets wet. The ads were filled with complicated abbreviations for amenities I would never need. And then I saw this:

"One Bedroom Apartment. Hardwood Floors. Quiet."

I called the number in the ad and a woman answered. Her voice was friendly and warm and you could hear people talking in the background. She asked if I wanted to come and see the apartment.

—No, I said.

I told her I was coming from New England but that I hoped to be in Los Angeles soon. She said she had always wanted to go to New England but family had always kept her in Los Angeles. There was wistfulness in her voice and I wondered if she thought some part of her lived in the seasons too. She asked if I had grown up in New England and I told her no, I had grown up in Los Angeles and had come east four years earlier. She asked if I missed my family, being so far away.

—Yes, I miss my family every day but you get used to it after awhile, I lied.

I didn't tell her my family was gone; you can't tell a stranger you don't have any family—that part of you disappeared before you left Los Angeles and now you're invisible and your whole heart has fallen out.

She asked me when I had seen my family last. I told her I hadn't seen them since I left. She said that just wasn't right and they must miss me as much as I missed them and that people shouldn't just go on missing each other forever. She told me that family was the most important thing there was.

—And love, I said.

—But the people we love become our family and so it's all the same thing.

—Yes, they do, I agreed.

But it's *not* the same thing.

When we are born, most of us have a family we would not have chosen. They are flawed and their flaws are sharp. They have the sort of soul that has to wander when we wish they had the sort of soul that loved us so much nothing could tear them away. Then they are gone and we don't know where they went or why they wanted to go or why they won't come back. And then there are people who come and our hearts choose them and their hearts choose us and they are flawed and their flaws are perfect. They love us so much nothing could tear them away. Then they are gone and we don't know where they went, but we know they can't come back even though they didn't want to go.

The woman asked me if I had been looking for an apartment long. I told her I had only decided that morning to come back.

—Ah, you must miss your family more today than other days.

—Something like that, I replied.

She told me her daughter was about to have a baby and she was going to be a grandmother. She said it was the happiest she'd ever been. She said she'd been busy preparing a nursery for the baby and asked if I wanted to see photos of the apartment. I told her no. She said she supposed that meant I didn't want to live there.

—That's not it, I just don't want to look at any photographs.

She said I seemed nice and that I sounded sad, like something was the matter and I needed to be with my family. I told her she was probably right. She said I could come and live there. She gave me the address.

17

The first morning I was back in Los Angeles, I heard the boy and his father in the alley. I had just woken and said good morning. The boy couldn't walk yet and his father was carrying him. The father's footsteps sounded like Finley's and for a moment I thought my heart was coming back to me. I jumped from my bed and walked to the window. That was when I saw them. That was when I knew my heart was not coming back to me.

When your heart falls out, sometimes it comes back quickly and sometimes it takes a long time. Other times it disappears for good. I think sometimes when you disappear, it is too hard to come back.

The window was dusty and the boy was small but I could tell by the way he moved his arms that if his father set him on his feet he would try to walk. He would take a few shaky steps and fall then look to his father's face for clues. If his father laughed he would smile and if he looked scared, the boy would cry.

When you are alone, the only place you can search for clues is the hole where your heart used to be.

For three years I've been alone in Los Angeles, watching the world through windows that are sometimes dusty and sometimes clear, listening to the outside and searching the hole where my heart used to be for clues.

18

I looked over at Finley's camera. It was manual; the sort of camera where you need to use your hands to make adjustments, to focus, to see clearly. The sort of camera where you hear the click and roll of the film, where you hear which moments are being chosen forever. I put your book of dreams in my bag and Finley's camera over my shoulder, across my heart. I pressed it to my chest and opened the door. The world was quiet as though I knew something no one else did when the flutter carried me outside. I walked across the balcony, down the stairs and out of the gate into the alley. In the alley behind my house there are large cracks in the asphalt and places where the gravel has come loose. I saw a dandelion bloom growing in the cracks and took a picture. I heard the familiar click and roll of the film.

I walked through the alley, heading in the direction the ocean bird had gone that day, listening to the sounds of the city waking after the rain. I stopped to watch myself in oil-slick rainbows, looking at my surrealist reflection and searching for my smile. I walked toward the street, toward the café and the people. I wasn't going to the café but when I walked past, I saw the boy and his father. Outside there was a young girl in a yellow dress holding a brown and white puppy on a leash. The puppy was pulling as far as he could and the girl was standing still. Inside, the boy was pointing at the girl and the puppy. I opened the door of the café and walked inside. I walked toward the line where the boy and his father stood. The father looked at me, but did not say *hello*. He was silent.

—Good morning, I whispered.

He looked at me. His look said something like: *I know the way it feels to want to forget. I know what it feels like to disappear and think your heart will never come back to you*. I went and stood at the back of the line. I watched the little boy. His hair has grown darker. His bowl cut was a little long and hung over his eyes. He pointed at the puppy, chattering animatedly to his father. I couldn't understand what he was saying, but I knew that he was happy. There is a special language that only parents and children can understand, it must have been that language. I left the café. I didn't want any coffee, I just wanted to know that all was right in the world.

I didn't take your book of dreams out of my bag when I went for my walk. I didn't go sit on the footbridge in the park and read it. I just wanted to know that it was there. I just wanted to know that I could. It seems like it's been so long since I knew anything.

When I came home, I walked through the alley again. I thought I would sit and watch the dandelion a moment. To marvel at the way wishes can bloom through cracks in asphalt. The dandelion was gone. No bloom. Only stem. It didn't matter. I had captured the dandelion forever. That wish was mine to keep, even though it was gone now. Just because it is gone now, that doesn't mean it wasn't real.

I took a picture of the empty stem. I looked at my surrealist reflection.

19

In Los Angeles there is no winter and there is no autumn. You don't always notice the passage of time. I mark time by the voices of the children next door and the games they play. I mark time by the boy and his father, by the baby and the wind chimes. The families around me change, the children grow but no matter how many days I watch the world through my windows, the leaves are always the same.

Sometimes I forget how long it has been since someone said 'I love you.' Three years is a long time between *I love yous*. It is hard to know how much time has passed when the world outside stays the same and no matter how many days you search the hole where your heart used to be, it is still empty. No matter how much I search, there are no clues.

Until this morning, I didn't think it was ever coming back to me. This morning I was looking out the window, watching the leaves and wishing they would change so I would know autumn was here. When I took the box down from the closet and found your book of dreams, I held it for a long time. I don't remember putting it in the box when I left New England. When I opened it, sheets of Finley's music fell out. I looked at the pieces of him, at his camera and the music he wrote. I wondered if some part of him knew he was disappearing that day when he said goodbye and walked out of the door and into the rain, if he felt his heart fall out and knew that mine would fall out too and so he left pieces of his heart in your book. I wonder if he hid them there so one day they would fall into my hands.

I searched the box for my heart and it wasn't there.

I looked outside and the leaves were the same. I held the song that was my name. The wind came, I heard the leaves rustle and the wind chimes played music that sounded like the song.

It is hard to know that autumn is here when you can't see it. The leaves don't change and so I don't know what to call it. You can't say autumn when the leaves don't change, but I heard the leaves and the song and felt a flutter where my heart used to be.

20

I thought about continuing my walk, about taking Finley's camera to the store, about saying hello to the stranger who delivered forever moments to people day after day, and about my fingertips grazing their palm when I put the roll of film in their hands. I thought that maybe I would look through the photographs one by one, see what Finley saw when he looked at me and remember my smile.

I came back to my apartment and opened your book of dreams again. I was lying on the floor next to my easel, reading when I came across one I hardly remember anything but the end of. In the end it said, *"This, our one hope for survival, our only hope to escape was sinking. Everybody watched us as we drifted into the current, drowning. Nobody was helping, nobody was moving. I took a picture..."*

Sometimes we think people are our only chance for survival. When Finley appeared and my heart came back to me, I thought he was my one chance for survival. I asked him if he loved me.

—Every day until forever, he said.

I thought forever wouldn't come for a long, long time. Maybe when we had children who were grown and never had to know what it feels like when your parents don't love each other anymore, never had to wonder if they were the reason one of them left. Maybe when there were love note reminders around the house telling him to order oil for the furnace before winter came and for me to turn off the fire under the kettle when I made our tea. I thought forever would be when he had written me enough songs and I enough love letters to him that if we spent the rest of our lives playing and reading, we would never finish before forever came. I thought that Finley had saved me and forever would come when we were old and had filled our home with enough love to save the world. I didn't know that when forever came for Finley and me it was only *that* forever that was over, that when he walked me home in the rain and my heart fell from the sky and came back to me, he hadn't saved me. He had just reminded me I was alive.

I didn't know that sometimes forever starts all over again.

That was when I read the dream about drowning and when you took a picture. I closed my eyes to search the hole where my heart used to be, but it was full. I pictured your words. That's when I noticed the ellipses at the end...

Special Thanks (in alphabetical order, mostly.)

Rafael Alvarado, William Brandon, Kela Brousard, Crystal Couch, Ryan Kirk, Quentin Kirk, Kristen McDermott, Erech Overaker, Jon Reed, Kimberly Sadler, Kevin Staniec, Twitter.

Eluvium, for creating *An Accidental Memory in the Case of Death*, the music this story was written to.

... and my Father, the first man who ever loved me.

Corrie Greathouse (corriegreathouse.com) is a writer, reformed relocater, founding member of the Hollywood Institute of Poetics, runner, volunteer, lover of twitter, and fan of the Oxford comma. She has read with Poets Laureate, featured across the country from NYC's Bowery Poetry Club to her favorite LA bookstore, Skylight Books, Pasadena's Vroman's, Barnes & Noble, and Beyond Baroque Literary Arts Center. Her work has been published in The *Toronto Quarterly*, *Falling Star Magazine*, and *Still Developing: A Story of Instant Gratification*.

Recognized by the City of Los Angeles for her work bringing literary arts to the community, she also volunteers tutoring homeless children through School on Wheels, and works with aspiring readers as part of the Adult Literacy Program of the Los Angeles Public Library.

She has no pets and got her first plants in 2012. She went away to write, came back, and they were dead.

Born and raised in Orange County, CA, she currently resides in Los Angeles.

Kim Sadler is an Editor/Writer at the Getty Museum in Los Angeles. She graduated from UC Santa Barbara with an English degree. While in Santa Barbara (where she left her heart) she wrote for The Daily Nexus and The Independent. She also works as a freelance editor, along with working on her own writing projects on the side. Kim enjoys sunshine, music, and the great outdoors, and does her best to get out of the city and into nature as often as she can.

Mark Smith (marksmithillustration.com) is a freelance illustrator and occasionally lectures on the BA Illustration course at Plymouth University in England. He has worked for magazines, newspapers and publishers around the world, including Penguin Books, Simon and Schuster, Hachette, The Folio Society, The Financial Times, The New York Times, The New Yorker, The Guardian, The Times, The Washington Post, ESPN, and many more. His images have also won recognition from the New York Society of Illustrators, LA Society of Illustrators, Communication Arts, 3X3 Pro Show, Association Of Illustrators, American Illustration, Creative Quarterly, and Creativity International. When he's not working, Mark likes to improve his throwing technique by throwing a ball for his dog Oscar who never, ever retrieves it.

BLACK HILL PRESS
Contemporary American Novellas
blackhillpress.com

Black Hill Press is a publishing collective founded on collaboration. Our growing family of writers and artists are dedicated to the novella—a distinctive, often overlooked literary form that offers the focus of a short story and the scope of a novel. We believe a great story is never defined by its length.

Annually, our independent press produces four quarterly collections of Contemporary American Novellas. Books are available in both print and digital formats, online and in your local bookstore, library, museum, university gift shop, and selected specialty accounts. Discounts are available for book clubs and teachers.

facebook.com/blackhillpress
flickr.com/ blackhillpress
instagram.com/blackhillpress
pinterest.com/ blackhillpress
twitter.com/ blackhillpress
vimeo.com/ blackhillpress
youtube.com/ blackhillpress